Troll
**Teacher
Time
Savers**

Arithmetic Fun

Reproducible Activity Sheets for Grades 2-3

Troll Associates

Troll Teacher Time Savers provide a quick source of self-contained lessons and practice material, designed to be used as full-scale lessons or to make productive use of those precious extra minutes that sometimes turn up in the day's schedule.

Troll Teacher Time Savers can help you to prepare a made-to-order program for your students. Select the sequence of Time Savers that will meet your students' needs, and make as many photocopies of each page as you require. Since Time Savers include progressive levels of complexity and difficulty in each book, it is possible to individualize instruction, matching the needs of each student.

Those who need extra practice and reinforcement for catching up in their skills can benefit from Troll Teacher Time Savers, while other students can use Time Savers for enrichment or as a refresher for skills in which they haven't had recent practice. Time Savers can also be used to diagnose a student's knowledge and skills level, in order to see where extra practice is needed.

Time Savers can be used as homework assignments, classroom or small-group activities, shared learning with partners, or practice for standardized testing. See "Answer Key & Skills Index" to find the specific skill featured in each activity.

ANSWER KEY & SKILLS INDEX

Page 1, **On the Farm:** 1-8; 2-7; 3-6; 4-21. **(counting)**

Page 2, **Hooray for the Parade:** 1-5; 2-5. **(single-digit addition word problems, no carrying)**

Page 3, **Horns, Flags & Drums:** 1-10; 2-8; 3-9. **(single-digit addition word problems, no carrying)**

Page 4, **The Magic Wand:** top, l to r-19, 14; middle, l to r-18, 15, 12, 17, 17; bottom, t to b-11, 16, 12. **(single-digit addition, no carrying)**

Page 5, **Writing Numbers Work-Out:** riddle answer-a coin. **(counting)**

Page 6, **Let's Go to the Zoo!:** 1-10; 2-4; 3-15. **(single-digit addition/subtraction word problems, no carrying or regrouping)**

Page 7, **Grandma's Coming!:** 1: 2+2+2+2+1=9; 2: 4+3+2=9; 3: 1+1+1+1+1+1=6. **(single-digit addition word problems, no carrying)**

Page 8, **Magic Marty:** top, l to r-5, 4, 7, 0, 2, 4; bottom, l to r-1, 3, 8, 6, 7, 9. **(single-digit subtraction, no borrowing)**

Page 9, **A Rope Trick:** t to b-4, 6, 2, 5, 7, 4; l to r-1, 3, 0, 8. **(single-digit subtraction, no borrowing)**

Page 10, **Marty & Maggie:** t to b-2, 4, 3, 6, 3, 8, 8, 9; l to r-1, 4, 0, 0, 4, 4, 10, 5, 10, 9, 4, 9. **(subtraction, no borrowing)**

Page 11, **Silly Silks:** 18-4 should be circled; 1st row, l to r-11, 14, 12, 12, 11, 12; 2nd row-13, 11, 14, 10, 12, 14; 3rd row-15, 12, 12, 13, 13, 13. **(subtraction, no borrowing)**

Page 12, **Round & Round:** **(multiplying by 2)**

Page 13, **Times Table:** **(multiplying by 3)**

Page 14, **How Many Times Is That?:** 1st row, l to r-6, 4, 16, 15, 6; 2nd row-4, 14, 12, 12, 6. **(single-digit multiplication)**

Page 15, **A New Twist:** 29 is 2 tens 9 ones; 47 is 4 tens 7 ones; 12 is one tens 2 ones; 55 is 5 tens 5 ones; 70 is 7 tens 0 ones; 74 is 7 tens 4 ones; 1st row, l to r-2 tens 2 ones; 8 tens 3 ones; 2nd row-9 tens 0 ones; 5 tens 1 ones; 3rd row-4 tens 6 ones; 7 tens 5 ones; 4th row-1 tens 9 ones; 6 tens 6 ones. **(place value)**

Page 16, **One to Ten:** top-3 tens 6 ones is 2 tens 16 ones; 7 tens 3 ones is 6 tens 13 ones; 5 tens 2 ones is 4 tens 12 ones; 4 tens 9 ones is 3 tens 19 ones; 3 tens 0 ones is 2 tens 10 ones; 1 tens 0 ones is 0 tens 10 ones; bottom-4 tens 13 ones; 2 tens 12 ones; 3 tens 11 ones; 1 tens 14 ones. **(place value)**

Page 17, **The Marching Band:** 1st row, l to r-58, 78; 2nd row-89, 79; 3rd row-98, 87, 82; 4th row-89, 79, 98, 98; 27+52 should be circled. **(two-digit addition, no carrying)**

Page 18, **Vicky Goes on Vacation:** 2: 42+23=65; 3: 3+5+2+2=12; 4: 4+2+3+5=14. **(addition word problems, no carrying)**

Page 19, **Beat That Drum:** 1st row, l to r-79, 56, 48, 45, 99; 2nd row-79, 98, 97; 3rd row-76, 64; 33+12 should be circled. **(two-digit addition, no carrying)**

Page 20, **Nursery Rhyme Time:** 2: 12-5=7; 3: 6+7=13; 4: 7-4=3. **(addition/subtraction word problems, no carrying)**

Page 21, **Three Cheers for Ears:** 1st row, l to r-11, 22; 2nd row-51, 12; 3rd row-14, 10, 41, 47, 43; 4th row-61, 15, 22, 14, 23; 5th row-35, 24, 61, 32, 34. **(subtraction, no borrowing)**

Page 22, **Stepping High:** 1-56; 2-34; 3-72. **(word problems, addition with carrying)**

Page 23, **Too Many Tubas:** 21+69 should be circled; 1st row, l to r-57, 90, 70, 90; 2nd row-91, 92, 91, 90. **(addition with carrying)**

Page 24, **Queen of the Parade:** 39+58 should be circled; 1st row, l to r-64, 62, 50, 97, 50; 2nd row-72, 92, 92, 73, 82. **(addition with carrying)**

Page 25, **Free Balloons:** clockwise from l-37; 97; 85; 99; 80; 87; 62; 92. **(addition with carrying)**

Page 26, **Rolling Along:** 1-55; 2-37; 3-38. **(addition word problems with carrying)**

Page 27, **Planning for Passover:** 1: 14+5=19; 2: 19+19=38; 3: 14+14+5= 33; 4: 19+19=38. **(addition word problems with carrying)**

Page 28, **Double Feature:** 1st row, l to r-1, 6; 2nd row-37, 88, 26; 3rd row-49, 15, 46; 4th row-18, 54, 63, 58. **(subtraction with borrowing)**

Page 29, **Magic Cards:** 1-45; 2-27; 3-17; 4-48. **(subtraction word problems with borrowing)**

Page 30, **Fred's Farm Animals:** 1-11; 2-10; 3-3; 4-12. **(addition/subtraction word problems with regrouping)**

Page 31, **A Day at the Toy Store:** 1-33 cents; 2-14 treasures; 3-34 dollars; 4-13 players; 5-31 cards; toy racing cars. **(reverse order subtraction, word problems)**

Page 32, **Disappearing Tricks:** 1-22; 2-42; 3-11. **(subtraction word problems, no borrowing)**

Page 33, **Fun at the Playground:** 2: 6+9=15 children; 3: 11-3=8 girls; 4: 6+2=8 children. **(addition/subtraction word problems with regrouping)**

Page 34, **Beach-Time Fun:** 1: 41-16=25 more snail shells; 2: 11-8=3 inches taller; 3: 23-17=6 more points. **(subtraction word problems with borrowing)**

Page 35, **Something Is Missing:** 1st row, l to r-9, 27, 7, 26, 18, 8; 2nd row-17, 14, 77, 38, 13, 49; 3rd row-25, 18, 48, 29, 14, 36. **(two-digit subtraction with borrowing)**

Page 36, **The Wheel Goes Round:** (multiplying by 5)

Page 37, **Who Broke the Yolk?:** 1-68, 2-12, 3-17. **(two-digit subtraction word problems with borrowing)**

Page 38, **Super Saw:** 1st row, l to r-26, 57, 29, 19, 29; 2nd row-6, 35, 18, 18, 14; 3rd row-58, 57, 19, 29, 37. **(two-digit subtraction with borrowing)**

Page 39, **Everything in Its Place:** top-254 is 2 hundreds 5 tens 4 ones; 306 is 3 hundreds 0 tens 6 ones; 599 is 5 hundreds 9 tens 9 ones; 672 is 6 hundreds 7 tens 2 ones; 410 is 4 hundreds 1 tens 0 ones; 163 is 1 hundreds 6 tens 3 ones; bottom- 1 hundreds 5 tens 1 ones; 3 hundreds 9 tens 7 ones; 8 hundreds 3 tens 8 ones; 2 hundreds 0 tens 3 ones; 9 hundreds 1 tens 4 ones; 5 hundreds 4 tens 0 ones; 4 hundreds 6 tens 2 ones; 1 hundreds 1 tens 9 ones; 6 hundreds 7 tens 6 ones. **(place value)**

Page 40, **Place-Value Patchwork:** top row, l to r-blue, green, brown, green; 2nd row-purple, orange, pink, yellow; 3rd row-red, pink, brown, red; bottom row-orange, blue, yellow, purple. **(place value)**

Page 41, **Color the Calendar:** 1-Fri.; 2-Feb. 11; 3-Feb. 28; 4-Feb. 18; 5-4; 6-16; 7-19; 8-89 days. **(calendar skills)**

Page 42, **Reading Numbers Round-Up:** A-79; B-96; C-101; D-208; E-311; F-439; G-842; H-1,002; I-2,200; J-4,091; K-7,440; L-9,658. **(place value)**

Page 43, **Firefighter Fun:** 1st row, l to r-578, 374, 979, 887; 2nd row-274, 597, 887; 3rd row-889, 628, 856; 174+200 should be circled. **(three-digit addition, no carrying)**

Page 44, **Cowboys & Cowgirls:** 1st row, l to r-926, 950; 2nd row-568, 790; 3rd row-969, 809; 4th row-440, 839; 5th row-781, 760; 440 cowgirls and cowboys. **(three-digit addition with carrying)**

Page 45, **We Love a Parade:** 1-720 people; 2-300 balloons; 3-400 twirlers and flag holders. **(three-digit addition word problems with carrying)**

Page 46, **Flying Balloons:** 1-820 balloons; 2-319 spots; 3-976 times. **(three-digit addition word problems with carrying)**

Page 47, **Musical Fun:** top row, l to r-901, 911, 900, 932, 903; bottom row-522, 921, 702, 741, 301. **(three-digit addition with carrying)**

Page 48, **Here Come the Drums:** 1st row, l to r-729, 762, 927, 784, 918; 2nd row-564, 927, 918, 784, 783; 362+284+138 should be circled. **(three-digit column addition with carrying)**

Page 49, **What's for Sale?:** 1: 139+122+107=368; 2: 218+176+142= 536; 3: 138+277+115=530. **(three-digit column addition word problems with carrying)**

Page 50, **Happy Ending:** 1st row, l to r-912, 61; 2nd row-$7.99 886, $1.45; 3rd row-1135, 134, 71, 12; last row-88, 222, $9.90, 579. **(mixed addition with carrying)**

Page 51, **Clowning Around:** 1-$.85; 2-$1.37; 3-$.63. **(money addition word problems with carrying)**

Page 52, Funny Money: 1: $1.49+.75=$2.24; 2: $.77+.15=$.92; 3: $1.55 +1.49=$3.04; 4: $1.25+.65=$1.90; yes. **(money addition word problems with carrying)**

Page 53, Money Magic: 1: $5.00-2.55=$2.45 in change; 2: $7.36-3.97=$3.39 more for the red hat; 3: $6.52-3.68=$2.84 more for the big one; 4: $4.31-3.68=$.63 left. **(money subtraction word problems with borrowing)**

Page 54, At the Seashore: 1-2; 2-2; 3-3 **(mixed review, word problems)**

Page 55, Root for the Fruit: 1: 625-382=243; 2: 367-284=83; 3: 448-172=276. **(three-digit subtraction word problems with borrowing)**

Page 56, Just Passing Through: 1st row, l to r-209, 171, 329, 171, 391, 365; 2nd row-355, 195, 126, 153, 448, 66; 3rd row-385, 245; 4th row-467, 298; 5th row-28, 349. **(three-digit subtraction with borrowing)**

Page 57, Rabbit Snack: 241-158=83 should be circled; 1st row, l to r-360, 178, 377, 248, 134; 2nd row-203, 83, 391, 276, 778. **(three-digit subtraction with borrowing)**

Page 58, Take a Bow: 1st row, l to r-138, 179, 96, 518, 679; 2nd row-377, 387, 88, 279, 385. **(three-digit subtraction with borrowing)**

Page 59, Magic Paper Trick: 1: 536-387=149; 2: 425-279=146; 3: 924-857=67. **(three-digit subtraction word problems with borrowing)**

Page 60, Crossword Math: M-$3.14; U-22; S-196; I-30; A-48; B-$2.26; P-42; L-135; D-804; T-64; C-142; R-7; H-$9.00; Y-$3.00. **(mixed review)**

Page 61, Money Matters: 1: $10.99-1.99=$9.00; 2: $125.00-110.00=$15.00; 3: $15.00-3.00=$12.00; 4: $21.98-18.00=$3.98; 5: $18.00x5=$90.00. **(money subtraction with borrowing)**

Page 62, Let's Have a Party: 1: 10-6=4 boys; 2: 10x4=40 pieces; 3: 20-10=10 and 10-2=8 slices. **(mixed review word problems)**

Page 63, Birthday Balloons: 1: $1.85-1.52=$.33; 2: $2.49+1.39+.99=$4.87 and $5.00-4.87=$.13; 3: 40x.05=$2.00. **(money mixed review)**

Page 64, What's for Dinner?: 1: 6+6=12 chops and potatoes; 2: 4x6=24 asparagus; 3: 12+24=36 food items; 4: 4+2=6 left-over asparagus. **(mixed review word problems)**

Page 65, Mother's Day: 1: $1.75+3.95=$5.70; 2: $2.25+6.50=$8.75; 3: $5.99+2.25=$8.24; 4: choice 1; 5: $8.75-7.50=$1.25. **(money addition and subtraction word problems)**

Page 66, Dinosaur Doings: 1: $10.00-5.29=$4.71 (second dinosaur); 2: 23+48=71 and 122-71=51 (fourth dinosaur); 3: 132+132=264 and 264-57=207 (first dinosaur); 4: 60-26=34 (third dinosaur). **(mixed review word problems)**

Page 67, The Food Market: 1: 3x6=18 apples; 2: 4x2=8 ears of corn; 3: 2x9=18 and 2x6=12 and 18+12=30 grapes; 4: 4x6=24 cans; 5: 12x5=60 mini-pizza bagels. **(mixed review word problems)**

Page 68, Time Travels: 1-6:00 p.m.; 2-4:00 p.m.; 3-one hour; 4-6:45 p.m.; 5-5:40 p.m. **(telling time word problems)**

Page 69, Time Tricks: 1-4:20 p.m.; 2-one hour and fifteen minutes; 3-7:30 a.m.; 4-one hour. **(telling time word problems)**

Page 70, TV Time Troubles: 1-one hour; 2-borrow one hour of TV watching on Wednesday night so that he can watch two hours of hockey on Tuesday night; 3-four hours, more. **(telling time word problems)**

Page 71, Food Fun: 1: 4/8; 2: 1/3; 3: 1/4. **(fraction word problems)**

Page 72, Measurement Madness: 1: 8 pints+1 pint=9 pints of liquid; 2: 4 quarts-1 quart=3 quarts; 3: 2 feet+4 feet=6 feet and 6 feet divided by 3 feet=2 yards of countertop; 4: 48 inches divided by 12 inches=4 feet long. **(measurement word problems)**

Page 73, Roman Rules: IV is four; X is ten; I is one; VII is seven; XII is twelve; XVIII is eighteen; XV is fifteen; VI is six; III is three; II is two; XIII is thirteen; XI is eleven. **(Roman numbers)**

Page 74, Money Talks: 1-Luis must save his money for 2 weeks to buy his new cap; 2-Luis must save his money for 3 weeks to buy his CD; 3-Luis must save for 5 weeks to buy his sneakers. **(money word problems)**

On the Farm

There are many animals hidden in this picture. Find them and answer the questions below. Put your answers in the boxes.

1. How many birds are in the tree?

2. How many chickens are roosting in the barn?

3. How many horses are in the stable?

4. How many animals are there altogether?

Name_____ Date _____

Here comes the parade!

1. There are 4 people marching.
    There is 1 person standing.
    How many people are there in all?
    Write your answer in the box.

$$\begin{array}{r} 4 \\ +1 \\ \hline \end{array}$$

$$4 + 1 = \boxed{5}$$

2. There are 2 people with horns.
    There are 3 people without horns.
    How many people does that make?
    Write your answer in the box.

$$\begin{array}{r} 2 \\ +3 \\ \hline \end{array}$$

$$2 + 3 = \boxed{}$$

Name_____ Date _____

Horns, Flags & Drums

Write the answer in each box.

1. The red band has 5 horns.
   The blue band has 2 horns.
   The yellow band has 3 horns.
   How many horns in all?

$5 + 2 + 3 = \boxed{}$

$$\begin{array}{r} 5 \\ 2 \\ + 3 \\ \hline \boxed{} \end{array}$$

2. The red band has 3 flags.
   The blue band has 3 flags.
   The yellow band has 2 flags.
   How many flags in all?

$$\begin{array}{r} 3 \\ 3 \\ + 2 \\ \hline \boxed{} \end{array}$$

$3 + 3 + 2 = \boxed{}$

3. The red band has 2 drums.
   The blue band has 5 drums.
   The yellow band has 2 drums.
   How many drums in all?

$2 + 5 + 2 = \boxed{}$

$$\begin{array}{r} 2 \\ 5 \\ + 2 \\ \hline \boxed{} \end{array}$$

Name _____ Date _____

3

The Magic Wand

Find ten number problems here.
Write the answer
for each one.

$$3$$
$$7$$
$$+\ 9$$

$$8$$
$$+\ 6$$

$$9$$
$$+\ 9$$

$$2$$
$$5$$
$$+\ 8$$

$$6$$
$$+\ 6$$

$$4 + 6 + 7 =$$

$$4 + 9 + 4 =$$

$$6 + 5 =$$

$$8 + 8 =$$

$$7 + 5 =$$

Name _____ Date _____

Writing Numbers Work-Out

Write the missing numbers on the grid. Then count by 5's to do the dot-to-dot and discover the answer to the riddle. The first few numbers are done for you.

1	2	3	4	5					10					15					20
				25					30					35					40
				45					50					55					60
				65					70					75					80
				85					90					95					100
				105					110					115					120
				125					130					135					140
				145					150					155					160
				165					170					175					180
				185					190					195					200

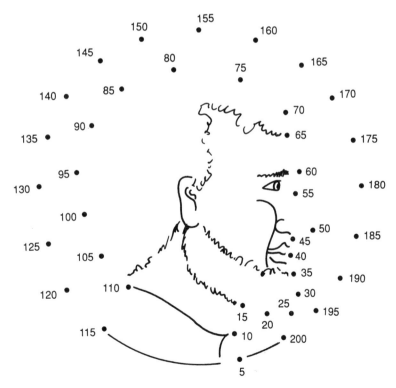

Dot-to-dot riddle: *What has a head and a tail, but no body?*

_____

Name _____ **Date** _____

Let's Go to the Zoo!

Every word problem has two parts. The first part *tells* you something. The second part *asks* you something. **Read each problem and fill in "Part 1" and "Part 2." Then solve the problem and write your answer on the blank.**

1. The zoo has 6 giraffes. It also has 4 elephants. How many giraffes and elephants does the zoo have altogether?

    Part 1:   The zoo has _____ giraffes.

    The zoo has _____ elephants.

    Part 2:   How many giraffes and elephants does the zoo have altogether?

    Answer: _____ giraffes and elephants

    $$\begin{array}{r} 6 \\ +\ 4 \\ \hline \end{array}$$

2. There were 9 tigers at the zoo. The zoo gave 5 tigers to the circus. How many tigers were left at the zoo?

    Part 1:   The zoo had _____ tigers.

    _____ tigers went to the circus.

    Part 2:   How many tigers were left at the zoo?

    Answer: _____ tigers

    $$\begin{array}{r} 9 \\ -\ 5 \\ \hline \end{array}$$

3. Dabney saw 7 blue parrots at the zoo. Then he saw 8 red parrots. How many parrots did Dabney see in all?

    Part 1:   Dabney saw _____ blue parrots.

    He saw _____ red parrots.

    Part 2:   How many parrots did Dabney see?

    Answer: _____ parrots

    $$\begin{array}{r} 7 \\ +\ 8 \\ \hline \end{array}$$

Name_____   **Date** _____

Grandma's Coming!

Write a number sentence (equation) under each word problem to find the answer.

1. Ricki's grandmother is coming to visit from the Phillipines. Ricki is helping Mother prepare Grandma's room. Ricki needs to find two pillowcases and two sheets, two bath towels and two washcloths, and one blanket in the linen closet. How many items does she need in all?

   _____ = [   ]

2. Grandma loves to read. Ricki goes to the library to find some good books and magazines to put in Grandma's room. She checks out four mysteries, three magazines, and two cookbooks. How many items does she check out altogether?

   _____ = [   ]

3. Ricki wants to make Grandma's favorite Filipino dish as a surprise. She needs a chicken, vinegar, soy sauce, peppercorns, and garlic. Mother says they need to buy rice, too. How many things are on Ricki's shopping list?

   _____ = [   ]

Name_____ **Date** _____

Fill in the answers.

6	7	9	8	6	8
−1	−3	−2	−8	−4	−4

4	7	9	8	8	9
−3	−4	−1	−2	−1	−0

Name_____ Date _____

A Rope Trick

Fill in the answers.

$9 - 5 =$

$8 - 2 =$

$5 - 3 =$

$9 - 4 =$

$9 - 2 =$

$7 - 3 =$

$6 - 5 =$

$6 - 6 =$

$7 - 4 =$

$9 - 1 =$

Name_____ Date _____

Marty & Maggie

Write the missing number in each box.

$4 - \boxed{} = 2$

$9 - \boxed{} = 5$

$10 - \boxed{} = 7$

$8 - \boxed{} = 2$

$\boxed{} - 2 = 1$

$\boxed{} - 5 = 3$

$\boxed{} - 4 = 4$

$\boxed{} - 3 = 6$

I'd like you to meet my assistant.

$$\begin{array}{r} 6 \\ -\,\boxed{} \\ \hline 5 \end{array} \qquad \begin{array}{r} 7 \\ -\,\boxed{} \\ \hline 3 \end{array} \qquad \begin{array}{r} 9 \\ -\,\boxed{} \\ \hline 9 \end{array} \qquad \begin{array}{r} 3 \\ -\,\boxed{} \\ \hline 3 \end{array} \qquad \begin{array}{r} 5 \\ -\,\boxed{} \\ \hline 1 \end{array} \qquad \begin{array}{r} 10 \\ -\,\boxed{} \\ \hline 6 \end{array}$$

$$\begin{array}{r} \boxed{} \\ -\,9 \\ \hline 1 \end{array} \qquad \begin{array}{r} \boxed{} \\ -\,3 \\ \hline 2 \end{array} \qquad \begin{array}{r} \boxed{} \\ -\,5 \\ \hline 5 \end{array} \qquad \begin{array}{r} \boxed{} \\ -\,7 \\ \hline 2 \end{array} \qquad \begin{array}{r} \boxed{} \\ -\,4 \\ \hline 0 \end{array} \qquad \begin{array}{r} \boxed{} \\ -\,5 \\ \hline 4 \end{array}$$

Name _____ **Date** _____

Silly Silks

Magic Marty should have 18 silk handkerchiefs in his pocket. But today 4 of them are in the wash. Which problem would help you find out how many silk handkerchiefs Magic Marty has in his pocket? Circle it. Then solve all the problems.

12	19	15	18	19	17
− 1	− 5	− 3	− 6	− 8	− 5

15	14	18	19	16	17
− 2	− 3	− 4	− 9	− 4	− 3

18	13	19	18	16	19
− 3	− 1	− 7	− 5	− 3	− 6

Name_____ Date _____

Round & Round

Look at the multiplication wheel. Multiply each number in the inner ring by the number in the center. Put your answer in the space in the outer ring.

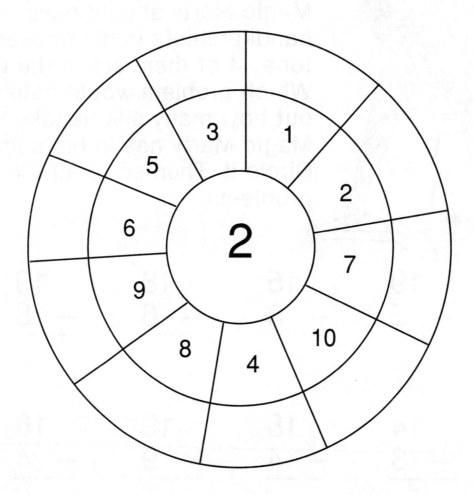

Name_____ Date _____

Times Table

Help to set the table by solving the problems.

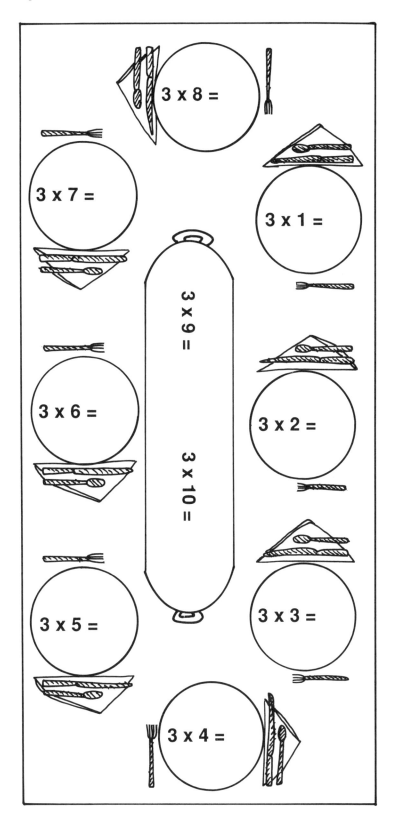

Name_____ **Date** _____

How Many Times Is That?

Solve the problems.

3	4	8	5	6
x 2	x 1	x 2	x 3	x 1

1	7	2	3	2
x 4	x 2	x 6	x 4	x 3

Name_____   Date _____

A New Twist

Draw a line from each number to the box that tells what the number means.

29

47

12

55

70

74

1 ten 2 ones

7 tens 4 ones

2 tens 9 ones

5 tens 5 ones

4 tens 7 ones

7 tens 0 ones

───── Write the number that goes in each space below. ─────

22 = _____tens _____ones

90 = _____tens _____ones

46 = _____tens _____ones

19 = _____tens _____ones

83 = _____tens _____ones

51 = _____tens _____ones

75 = _____tens _____ones

66 = _____tens _____ones

Name_____ Date _____

15

One to Ten

Draw a line from each box on the left to the one on the right that says the same thing in a different way. The first one has been done for you.
REMEMBER: 1 TEN = 10 ONES.

3 tens 6 ones	4 tens 12 ones
7 tens 3 ones	2 tens 10 ones
5 tens 2 ones	0 tens 10 ones
4 tens 9 ones	6 tens 13 ones
3 tens 0 ones	2 tens 16 ones
1 ten 0 ones	3 tens 19 ones

Fill in the spaces below.
The first one has been done to show you how.

5 tens 3 ones = ___4___ tens ___13___ ones

3 tens 2 ones = _____ tens _____ ones

4 tens 1 ones = _____ tens _____ ones

2 tens 4 ones = _____ tens _____ ones

Name_____ Date _____

The Marching Band

Fill in the answers.

$$27 + 31$$

$$42 + 36$$

$$54 + 35$$

$$50 + 29$$

$$34 + 64$$

$$44 + 43$$

$$52 + 30$$

$$22 + 67$$

$$27 + 52$$

$$75 + 23$$

$$14 + 84$$

The marching band has 27 short people and 52 tall people. Which number problem will help you find out how many people there are in all? Circle it.

Name_____ Date _____

Vicky Goes on Vacation

Write a number sentence (equation) on the line that will solve each word problem. Choose the correct answer from those in the car and write it in the box. The first one is done for you.

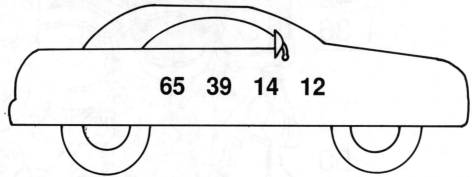

65 39 14 12

1. Vicky wants to take 4 coloring books and 35 crayons on her vacation. How many coloring items will she take?

    4 + 35 _____ = | **39** |

2. Vicky's parents have to pack a lot of vitamins for their family. They take 42 vitamins for Vicky and 23 vitamins for their son. How many total vitamins do Vicky's parents pack?

    _____ = | |

3. Vicky has three suitcases. Her brother has 5 suitcases. Their parents have 2 more suitcases each. How many suitcases does Vicky's family have altogether?

    _____ = | |

4. Vicky's family will be hungry on their trip. Her mother makes 4 ham sandwiches, 2 peanut butter sandwiches, 3 cheese sandwiches and 5 cream cheese sandwiches. How many sandwiches are made in all?

    _____ = | |

Name_____ **Date** _____

Beat That Drum

Fill in the answers.

66	35	16	33	48
+ 13	+ 21	+ 32	+ 12	+ 51

		56	73	35
		+ 23	+ 25	+ 62

			63	52
			+ 13	+ 12

There were 33 big drums and 12 small drums in the marching band. Which number problem will help you to find out how many drums there were all together? Circle it.

Name_____ **Date** _____

Nursery Rhyme Time

Read each word problem. Write a number problem and its answer in the correct nursery-rhyme picture. The first one is done for you.

1. First 3 cows jumped over the moon. Then 8 more cows jumped over the moon. How many cows jumped over the moon?

    _____3 + 8_____ = | 11 |

2. Peter Pumpkin Eater had 12 pumpkins. He ate 5 of them. How many pumpkins remained?

     = | |

3. Jack jumped over 6 candlesticks. Then Jack jumped over seven more. How many candlesticks did Jack jump over in all?

     = | |

4. Little Jack Horner had two plum pies. His first pie had 4 plums in it. His second pie had 7 plums. How many more plums did his second pie have?

     = | |

Name _____ **Date** _____

Three Cheers for Ears

Fill in the answers.

$$\begin{array}{r} 22 \\ -11 \\ \hline \end{array} \qquad \begin{array}{r} 47 \\ -25 \\ \hline \end{array}$$

$$\begin{array}{r} 68 \\ -17 \\ \hline \end{array} \qquad \begin{array}{r} 45 \\ -33 \\ \hline \end{array}$$

$$\begin{array}{r} 29 \\ -15 \\ \hline \end{array} \quad \begin{array}{r} 34 \\ -24 \\ \hline \end{array} \quad \begin{array}{r} 62 \\ -21 \\ \hline \end{array} \quad \begin{array}{r} 89 \\ -42 \\ \hline \end{array} \quad \begin{array}{r} 74 \\ -31 \\ \hline \end{array}$$

$$\begin{array}{r} 96 \\ -35 \\ \hline \end{array} \quad \begin{array}{r} 69 \\ -54 \\ \hline \end{array} \quad \begin{array}{r} 42 \\ -20 \\ \hline \end{array} \quad \begin{array}{r} 37 \\ -23 \\ \hline \end{array} \quad \begin{array}{r} 58 \\ -35 \\ \hline \end{array}$$

$$\begin{array}{r} 76 \\ -41 \\ \hline \end{array} \quad \begin{array}{r} 36 \\ -12 \\ \hline \end{array} \quad \begin{array}{r} 85 \\ -24 \\ \hline \end{array} \quad \begin{array}{r} 59 \\ -27 \\ \hline \end{array} \quad \begin{array}{r} 68 \\ -34 \\ \hline \end{array}$$

Name_____ **Date**_____

Stepping High

Fill in the answers.

1. The marchers in the parade wore hats. There were 28 yellow hats and 28 red hats. How many hats in all?

$$\begin{array}{r} 28 \\ + 28 \\ \hline \end{array}$$

2. When the marchers stopped to rest, 19 had drinks of soda, and 15 had drinks of juice. How many marchers had drinks in all?

$$\begin{array}{r} 19 \\ + 15 \\ \hline \end{array}$$

3. Pam threw her baton in the air 35 times. Joan threw her baton in the air 37 times. In all, how many times did Pam and Joan throw their batons in the air?

$$\begin{array}{r} 35 \\ + 37 \\ \hline \end{array}$$

Date _____

Too Many Tubas

One band had 21 tubas. Another band had 69 tubas. Which number problem will help you to find out how many tubas there are in all? Circle it.

Fill in the answers.

$$\begin{array}{r} 28 \\ +29 \\ \hline \end{array} \qquad \begin{array}{r} 67 \\ +23 \\ \hline \end{array} \qquad \begin{array}{r} 35 \\ +35 \\ \hline \end{array} \qquad \begin{array}{r} 78 \\ +12 \\ \hline \end{array}$$

$$\begin{array}{r} 24 \\ +67 \\ \hline \end{array} \qquad \begin{array}{r} 56 \\ +36 \\ \hline \end{array} \qquad \begin{array}{r} 72 \\ +19 \\ \hline \end{array} \qquad \begin{array}{r} 21 \\ +69 \\ \hline \end{array}$$

Name_____ Date _____

Queen of the Parade

On the float with the queen of the parade, there were 39 red flowers and 58 white flowers. Which number problem below will help you to find out how many flowers there were in all? Circle it.

Fill in the answers.

$$\begin{array}{r} 48 \\ +16 \\ \hline \end{array} \qquad \begin{array}{r} 34 \\ +28 \\ \hline \end{array} \qquad \begin{array}{r} 17 \\ +33 \\ \hline \end{array} \qquad \begin{array}{r} 39 \\ +58 \\ \hline \end{array} \qquad \begin{array}{r} 26 \\ +24 \\ \hline \end{array}$$

$$\begin{array}{r} 16 \\ +56 \\ \hline \end{array} \qquad \begin{array}{r} 49 \\ +43 \\ \hline \end{array} \qquad \begin{array}{r} 43 \\ +49 \\ \hline \end{array} \qquad \begin{array}{r} 35 \\ +38 \\ \hline \end{array} \qquad \begin{array}{r} 65 \\ +17 \\ \hline \end{array}$$

Name_____ Date _____

Free Balloons

The clown in the parade has 8 problems for you to solve.
Fill in the answers.

$$44 + 53$$

$$67 + 18$$

$$24 + 75$$

$$45 + 35$$

$$12 + 25$$

$$56 + 31$$

$$26 + 36$$

$$80 + 12$$

Name_____ Date _____

25

Rolling Along

Fill in the answers.

1. In the auto parade there were 14 cars built
   in 1900. There were 18 cars built in 1920.
   There were 23 cars built in 1920.
   How many cars were there altogether?

$$
\begin{array}{r}
14 \\
18 \\
+\ 23 \\
\hline
\end{array}
$$

2. There were 10 red cars. There were 15
   white cars. And 12 cars were blue. In all,
   how many cars were red, white, or blue?

$$
\begin{array}{r}
10 \\
15 \\
+\ 12 \\
\hline
\end{array}
$$

3. There were fat people in 18 cars. There
   were thin people in 9 cars. There were
   tall people in 11 cars. In all, how many
   cars had fat people, thin people, or tall
   people?

$$
\begin{array}{r}
18 \\
9 \\
+\ 11 \\
\hline
\end{array}
$$

Name _____ Date _____

Planning for Passover

Michael and Beth are helping their mother get ready for the seder, the Passover feast. Many friends and relatives are coming—fourteen adults and five children in all. Everyone will need a dinner plate, a soup plate, and knives, forks, and spoons.

1. How many dinner plates should Michael set out?

2. Michael's mother tells him to give everyone a soup spoon and a teaspoon. How many spoons is that altogether?

3. Beth is putting a wine glass and a water glass at each adult's place, and only a water glass at each child's place. How many glasses is she putting out altogether?

4. Beth's mother made enough matzah balls to put two in each bowl of soup. How many did she make?

Write each number problem here. Then write the answer.

1.	2.	3.	4.

Name_____ **Date** _____

Double Feature

Fill in the answers.

$$\begin{array}{r} 10 \\ -\ 9 \\ \hline \end{array}$$

$$\begin{array}{r} 10 \\ -\ 4 \\ \hline \end{array}$$

$$\begin{array}{r} 43 \\ -\ 6 \\ \hline \end{array}$$

$$\begin{array}{r} 92 \\ -\ 4 \\ \hline \end{array}$$

$$\begin{array}{r} 35 \\ -\ 9 \\ \hline \end{array}$$

$$\begin{array}{r} 56 \\ -\ 7 \\ \hline \end{array}$$

$$\begin{array}{r} 24 \\ -\ 9 \\ \hline \end{array}$$

$$\begin{array}{r} 51 \\ -\ 5 \\ \hline \end{array}$$

$$\begin{array}{r} 26 \\ -\ 8 \\ \hline \end{array}$$

$$\begin{array}{r} 62 \\ -\ 8 \\ \hline \end{array}$$

$$\begin{array}{r} 71 \\ -\ 8 \\ \hline \end{array}$$

$$\begin{array}{r} 64 \\ -\ 6 \\ \hline \end{array}$$

Name_____ Date _____

Magic Cards

Draw a line from the word problem to the number problem that matches it. Then solve the number problem and write the answer in the space.

1. Magic Marty had a set of 52 cards. One day 7 cards disappeared. How many cards did he have left?

    _____ cards

    $$\begin{array}{r} 23 \\ -\ 6 \\ \hline \end{array}$$

2. Magic Marty put 36 cards in his pocket. But he had a hole in his pocket, and 9 cards fell out. How many cards did he have left in his pocket?

    _____ cards

    $$\begin{array}{r} 52 \\ -\ 4 \\ \hline \end{array}$$

3. Magic Marty put 23 cards in his hat. But 6 cards vanished. How many cards did he have left in his hat?

    _____ cards

    $$\begin{array}{r} 52 \\ -\ 7 \\ \hline \end{array}$$

4. Magic Marty bought a new set of 52 cards. But he lost 4 of the new cards on the way home. How many new cards did he have left?

    _____ cards

    $$\begin{array}{r} 36 \\ -\ 9 \\ \hline \end{array}$$

Name_____ **Date** _____

Fred's Farm Animals

Pay attention to clue words in story problems. Words like *altogether, in all, total,* and *how many* signal addition problems. Words like *are left, how many more, how much larger,* and *remains* signal subtraction problems. **Read each word problem. Draw a line to the correct number problem. Write your answer on the dotted line.**

1. Justin's father Fred had 16 horses on his farm. He sold 5 of them. How many horses are left?

   _ _ _ _ _ _ _ _ horses

$$\begin{array}{r} 12 \\ -\ 9 \\ \hline \end{array}$$

2. Fred's pig had 4 piglets last year. Then she had 6 piglets this year. How many piglets did Fred's pig have altogether?

   _ _ _ _ _ _ _ _ piglets

$$\begin{array}{r} 16 \\ -\ 5 \\ \hline \end{array}$$

3. Fred owns 12 cows. A neighboring farm owns 9 cows. How many more cows did Fred's farm have?

   _ _ _ _ _ _ _ _ cows

$$\begin{array}{r} 5 \\ +\ 7 \\ \hline \end{array}$$

4. Five sheep were eating the grass in the East Meadow. Seven more were eating the grass in the West Meadow. How many sheep in total were eating the grass on Fred's farm?

   _ _ _ _ _ _ _ _ sheep

$$\begin{array}{r} 4 \\ +\ 6 \\ \hline \end{array}$$

Name_____ **Date** _____

A Day at the Toy Store

Sometimes subtraction word problems are written in a reverse-order pattern. Remember to subtract the smaller number from the larger number, no matter which number is stated first. **Solve the reverse-order subtraction problems, then find out what Tom wants from the toy shop.**

Key

13=T   14 =O   28=I   31=S   33=Y   34 =R   43=N   65=A   77=G   98=C

---

1. Luis spent 65 cents on baseball cards in the toy store. He had 98 cents when he went into the store. How much did Luis have left?

    _____ cents

2. Betsy found 14 treasures in the *Sunken Treasure* game. But there were 28 treasures in all. How many treasures were there left to find?

    _____ treasures

3. Andrew must pay 43 dollars in rent in a *Monopoly* game. He had 77 dollars. How much money will he have left after he pays his rent?

    _____ dollars

4. Sean lost 3 of his 16 chess players while playing the board game. How many chess players did he have left?

    _____ chess players

5. It took Lisa 21 cards to win in a *Po-ke-no* game. A deck of cards has 52 cards. How many cards did Lisa not need?

    _____ cards

At the toy store, Tom wants:

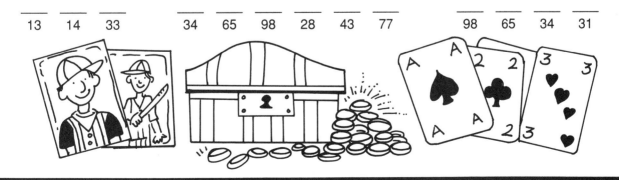

```
___  ___  ___      ___  ___  ___  ___  ___  ___      ___  ___  ___  ___
13    14   33       34   65   98   28   43   77       98   65   34   31
```

Name_____ Date _____

Disappearing Tricks

Read each word problem and decide which number problem you would use to find the answer. Solve it and write the answer on the line. Then cross out the other number problem.

1. Magic Marty took 38 rabbits out of his hat. But 16 rabbits hopped away. How many rabbits did he have left?

   $$38 - 16$$ $$16 - 38$$

   _____ rabbits

2. Magic Marty borrowed 75 gloves from people who came to his show. He made 33 gloves disappear. How many gloves did he have left?

   $$33 - 75$$ $$75 - 33$$

   _____ cards

3. Of the 75 people who let Magic Marty borrow their gloves, 64 said they would never let him borrow their gloves again. How many people would do it again?

   $$64 - 75$$ $$75 - 64$$

   _____ people

Name _____ Date _____

Fun at the Playground

**Read each word problem. Think about what the problem tells you.
Think about what the problem asks you. Next, put a box around the
correct number problem and solve it. Write your answer on the line.
Be sure to label your answer.** The first one is done for you.

1. There are 12 children throwing balls. Five children have had a turn throwing the ball.
    How many children have not thrown the ball yet?

    $$12 + 5$$

    $$12 - 5$$

    $$5 + 12$$

    7 children

2. Six boys are at the swings. Nine girls are at the swings. How many children are
    at the swings?

    $$6 + 9$$

    $$9 - 6$$

    $$6 - 9$$

3. Eleven children are jumping rope. Three of the children are boys. How many girls
    are jumping rope?

    $$3 - 11$$

    $$11 + 3$$

    $$11 - 3$$

4. Six boys have been tagged in a tag game. Two girls have been tagged.
    How many children have been tagged in all?

    $$6 + 2$$

    $$6 - 2$$

    $$2 - 6$$

Name_____ Date _____

Beach-Time Fun

Some subtraction and addition word problems ask you to compare two numbers. The question might be worded, *How much larger,* or *How many more.*
Read each word problem. Draw a line to the correct number sentence (equation). Solve the problem.

1. Tara found 41 snail shells and 16 clam shells in the sand. How many more snail shells than clam shells did Tara find?

$11 + 8 =$ ☐

$23 + 17 =$ ☐

$8 - 11 =$ ☐

$41 - 16 =$ ☐

2. Dominic measured the height of two sand castles he built. The first one was 8 inches tall. The second one was 11 inches tall. How much taller was Dominic's second sand castle than his first?

$23 - 17 =$ ☐

$11 - 8 =$ ☐

$16 - 41 =$ ☐

3. Amanda's beach-volleyball team scored 23 points. Adam's team scored 17 points. How many more points did Amanda's team score than Adam's?

$17 - 23 =$ ☐

$41 + 16 =$ ☐

Name_____ **Date** _____

34

Something Is Missing

Fill in the answers.

38 − 29	75 − 48	24 − 17	62 − 36	46 − 28	47 − 39
56 − 39	41 − 27	93 − 16	75 − 37	32 − 19	86 − 37
42 − 17	44 − 26	81 − 33	54 − 25	92 − 78	65 − 29

Name_____ Date _____

The Wheel Goes Round

Look at the multiplication wheel. Multiply each number in the inner ring by the number in the center. Put your answer in the space in the outer ring.

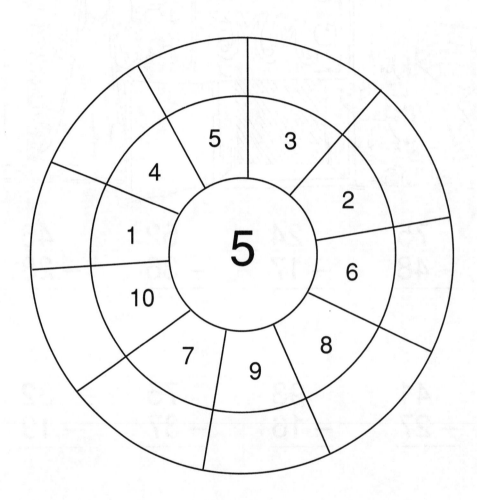

Name_____ **Date** _____

Who Broke the Yolk?

Draw a line from the word problem to the number problem that matches it.

Then solve the number problem and write the answer in the space.

1. Magic Marty had 83 eggs. He broke 15 of them. He put the rest into his hat. How many eggs did he put into his hat?

   _____ eggs

   $\begin{array}{r} 41 \\ -\ 29 \\ \hline \end{array}$

2. Magic Marty had 41 cups of milk. He poured 29 cups of milk into his hat. How many cups of milk did he have left?

   _____ cups

   $\begin{array}{r} 34 \\ -\ 17 \\ \hline \end{array}$

3. Magic Maggie took 34 of Magic Marty's eggs. But she broke 17 of them. How many eggs did she have left?

   _____ eggs

   $\begin{array}{r} 83 \\ -\ 15 \\ \hline \end{array}$

Name_____ Date _____

Super Saw

Fill in the answers.

51 − 25	72 − 15	67 − 38	31 − 12	45 − 16
64 − 58	74 − 39	31 − 13	56 − 38	42 − 28
77 − 19	83 − 26	35 − 16	48 − 19	62 − 25

Name _____ **Date** _____

Everything in Its Place

Draw a line from each number to the box that tells what the number means.

254

306

599

672

410

163

6 hundreds 7 tens 2 ones

1 hundred 6 tens 3 ones

2 hundreds 5 tens 4 ones

4 hundreds 1 tens 0 ones

3 hundreds 0 tens 6 ones

5 hundreds 9 tens 9 ones

Write the number that goes in each space below.

151 = _____ hundreds _____ tens _____ ones

397 = _____ hundreds _____ tens _____ ones

838 = _____ hundreds _____ tens _____ ones

203 = _____ hundreds _____ tens _____ ones

914 = _____ hundreds _____ tens _____ ones

540 = _____ hundreds _____ tens _____ ones

462 = _____ hundreds _____ tens _____ ones

119 = _____ hundreds _____ tens _____ ones

676 = _____ hundreds _____ tens _____ ones

Name_____ Date _____

Place-Value Patchwork

Use the code to color the patchwork quilt.

If the number in the quilt has:

9 hundreds, color it blue
7 ones, color it green
5 tens, color it yellow
4 hundreds, color it pink
2 tens, color it red
1 thousand, color it purple
8 tens, color it orange
3 ones, color it brown

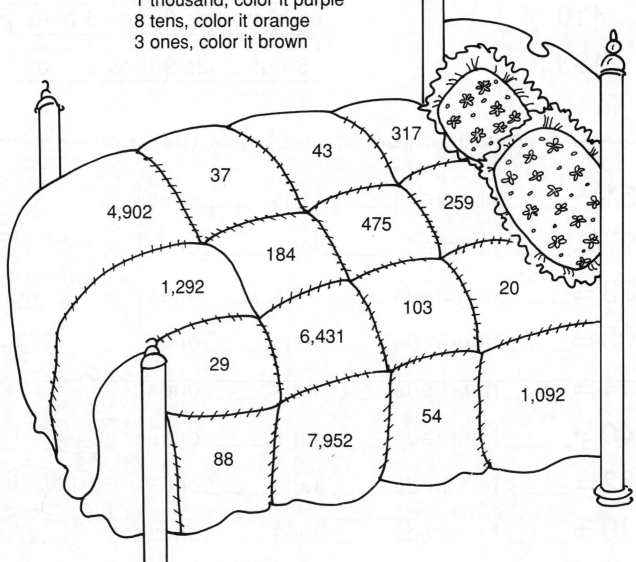

Name_____ Date _____

Color the Calendar

**Look at the calendar to help you answer the following questions.
You will need crayons for some of the answers.**

FEBRUARY						
Sunday	Monday	Tuesday	Wednesday	Thursday	Friday	Saturday
			1	2	3	4
5	6	7	8	9	10	11
12 Lincoln's Birthday	13	14 Valentine's Day	15	16	17	18
19	20 Presidents' Day	21	22 Washington's Birthday	23	24	25
26	27	28				

1. What day of the week is the 3rd day of February? Color the correct day-of-the-week box *blue*.

2. What date will it be 5 days from February 6? Color the date box *green*.

3. What date is 2 weeks from February 14? Color the date box *yellow*.

4. What date is the 3rd Saturday of February? Color the date box *red*.

5. How many Sundays are there in February? _____

6. How many days is it from February 7 to February 23? _____

7. If school is closed for Presidents' Day, how many school days are there in this February calendar? _____

8. If there are 28 days in February, 31 days in March, and 30 days in April, how many days are there in all 3 months? _____

Name_____ Date _____

Reading Numbers Round-Up

Read the number words. Write the *number* on the ferris wheel chair.

A. seventy-nine

B. ninety-six

C. one hundred one

D. two hundred eight

E. three hundred eleven

F. four hundred thirty-nine

G. eight hundred forty-two

H. one thousand two

I. two thousand two hundred

J. four thousand ninety-one

K. seven thousand four hundred forty

L. nine thousand six hundred fifty-eight

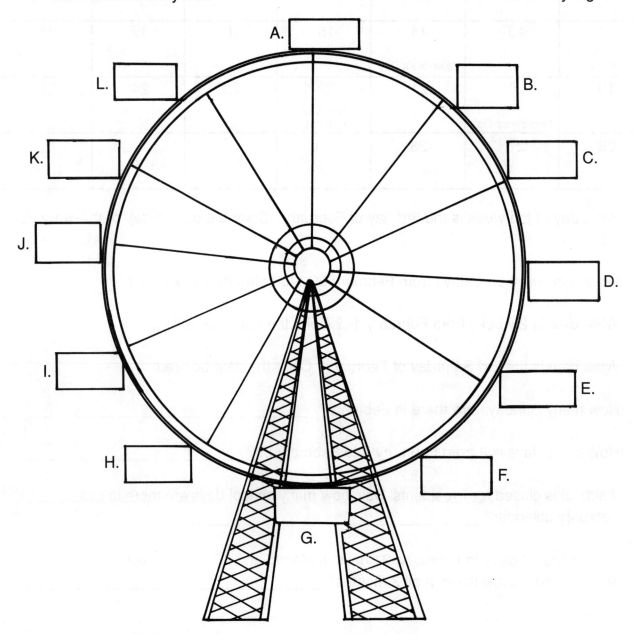

Name_____ **Date** _____

42

Firefighter Fun

Fill in the answers.

253 + 325	174 + 200	631 + 348	566 + 321
	152 + 122	393 + 204	566 + 321
	475 + 414	305 + 323	734 + 122

The firefighters put out 174 fires last year. They put out 200 fires this year. Which number problem above will help you find out how many fires there were in all? Circle it.

Name _____

Date _____

Cowboys & Cowgirls

Fill in the answers.

```
  134        819
+ 792      + 131


  193        445
+ 375      + 345


  685        321
+ 284      + 488


  218        256
+ 222      + 583


  558        329
+ 223      + 431
```

There were 218 cowgirls in the parade. There were 222 cowboys. All together how many cowgirls and cowboys were there? _____

Name_____ Date _____

We Love a Parade

Fill in the answers.

1. At the parade there were 364 people on one side of the street and 356 people on the other side. How many people came to the parade?

$$\begin{array}{r} 364 \\ + 356 \\ \hline \end{array}$$

2. There were 125 yellow balloons sold at the parade. There were 175 red balloons sold. How many balloons were sold in all?

$$\begin{array}{r} 125 \\ + 175 \\ \hline \end{array}$$

3. Joan counted 275 twirlers in the parade. Joe counted 125 flag holders. In all, how many twirlers and flag holders were there?

$$\begin{array}{r} 275 \\ + 125 \\ \hline \end{array}$$

Name _____   Date _____

Flying Balloons

Fill in the answers.

1. There were big and small balloons in the
   parade. There were 639 small balloons.
   There were 181 big balloons. How many
   balloons were there in all?

      639
   + 181
   _____

2. The giraffe balloon had 162 spots on
   one side, and 157 spots on the other
   side. How many spots were there in all?

      162
   + 157
   _____

3. The people who held the flying giraffe
   waved 744 times with their right hands
   and 232 times with their left hands. How
   many times did they wave in all?

      744
   + 232
   _____

Name_____ Date _____

Musical Fun

Fill in the answers.

567	679	743	683	318
+ 334	+ 232	+ 157	+ 249	+ 585

364	282	346	289	135
+ 158	+ 639	+ 356	+ 452	+ 166

Here Come the Drums

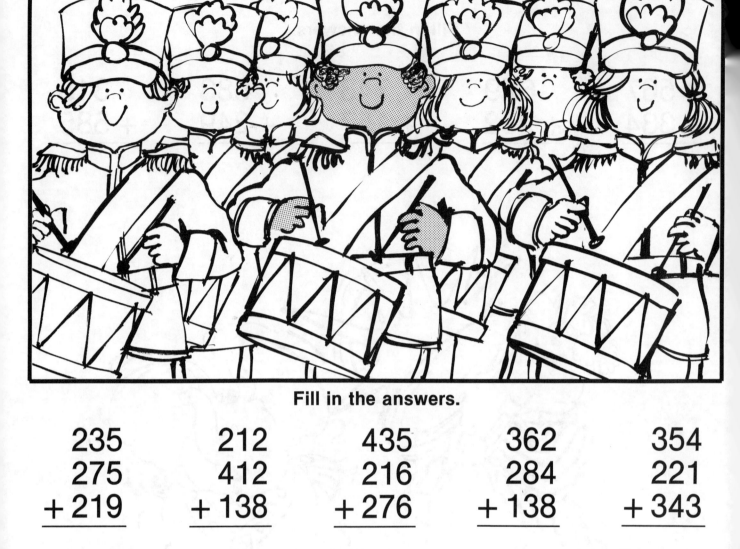

Fill in the answers.

```
  235        212        435        362        354
  275        412        216        284        221
+ 219      + 138      + 276      + 138      + 343
```

```
  284        276        354        362        240
  163        216        221        284        405
+ 117      + 435      + 343      + 138      + 138
```

In the marching band, Larry hit his drum 362 times.
Barbara hit her drum 284 times and Sam hit his drum
138 times. Find the number problem that shows how
many times they hit their drums in all. Circle it.

Name_____ Date _____

What's for Sale?

Write each number
problem here. ⇦
Then write the answer.

1. Mrs. Jones sold drinks at the parade. She
   sold 139 cups of lemonade, 122 cups of
   orange drink and 107 cups of fruit
   punch. How many drinks did Mrs. Jones
   sell in all?

2. Mr. Todd sold 218 flags, 176 buttons and
   142 pinwheels. How many things did he
   sell in all?

3. John sold peanuts. He sold 138 bags of
   peanuts before the parade, 277 bags
   during the parade, and 115 bags after
   the parade. How many bags of peanuts
   did John sell in all?

Name_____ Date _____

Happy Ending

At the end of the parade there were bright colored fireworks.
Fill in the answers. Then celebrate!

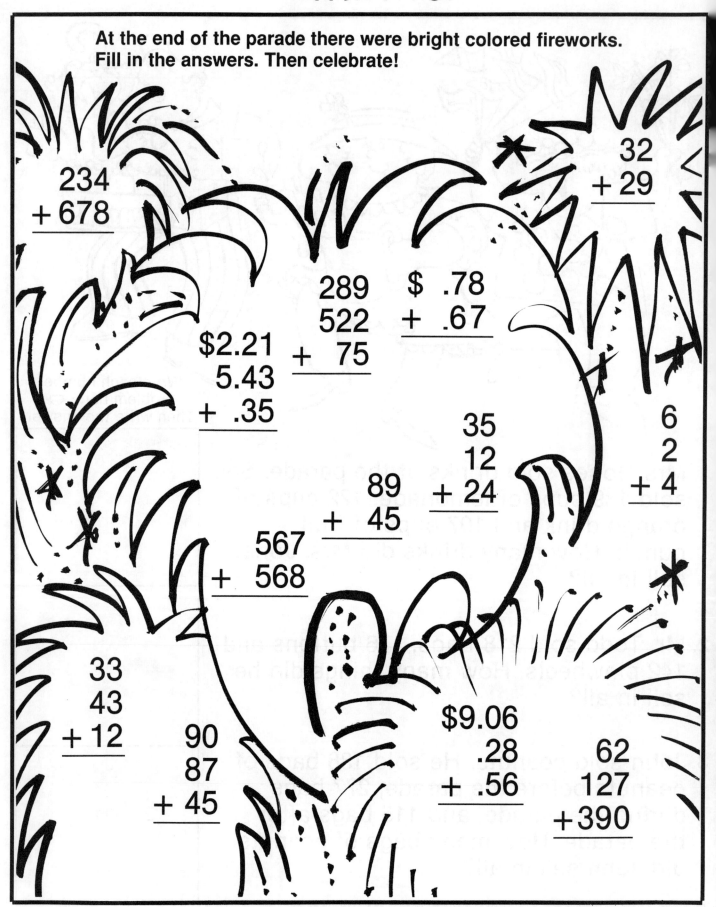

```
 234
+678
```

```
 32
+29
```

```
 289
 522
+ 75
```

```
$ .78
+ .67
```

```
$2.21
 5.43
+ .35
```

```
 35
 12
+24
```

```
 6
 2
+4
```

```
 89
+45
```

```
 567
+568
```

```
 33
 43
+12
```

```
 90
 87
+45
```

```
$9.06
  .28
+ .56
```

```
  62
 127
+390
```

Name_____ Date_____

Clowning Around

Fill in the answers.

1. Bozo spent 20 cents for a cookie and 65 cents for milk. How much money did he spend in all?

$$\begin{array}{r} \$\ .20 \\ +\ .65 \\ \hline \end{array}$$

2. Silly Sam had one dollar and 12 cents. Then he found 25 cents. How much did he have all together?

$$\begin{array}{r} \$1.12 \\ +\ .25 \\ \hline \end{array}$$

3. Funny Fran has 6 cents in one hand and 57 cents in the other. How much does she have in all?

$$\begin{array}{r} \$\ .06 \\ +\ .57 \\ \hline \end{array}$$

Name_____ Date _____

Funny Money

Draw a line from the word problem to the number problem that matches it. Then do the number problem.

$ .77
+ .15

1. Ann spent $1.49 for a big balloon and 75 cents for ice cream. How much did Ann spend all together?

$1.49
+ .75

2. Joe bought a small flag for 77 cents. Then he bought some punch that cost 15 cents. How much did Joe spend in all?

$1.25
+ .65

3. Beth bought her little sister a giant pinwheel for $1.55. She bought herself a big balloon for $1.49. How much did Beth spend in all?

$1.55
+1.49

4. Bob has $2.00. He wants to buy a flag for $1.25 and a drink of lemonade for 65 cents. How much will he have to spend all together?
Does Bob have enough money?

Write Yes or No. _____

Money Magic

Draw a line from the word problem to the number problem that matches it. Then do the number problem. Write the answer in the space.

1. Magic Marty bought rabbit food that cost $2.55. He gave the man $5.00. How much change did Magic Marty get?

$$\begin{array}{r} \$\ 7.36 \\ -\ 3.97 \\ \hline \end{array}$$

————

2. Magic Marty bought some new hats for his act. He spent $7.36 for a red one and $3.97 for a blue one. How much more did the red one cost than the blue one?

$$\begin{array}{r} \$\ 6.52 \\ -\ 3.68 \\ \hline \end{array}$$

————

3. A small saw costs $3.68. A large one costs $6.52. How much more does the big one cost than the small one?

$$\begin{array}{r} \$\ 4.31 \\ -\ 3.68 \\ \hline \end{array}$$

————

4. Magic Marty has $4.31 in his pocket. If he buys a small saw for $3.68, how much will he have left?

$$\begin{array}{r} \$\ 5.00 \\ -\ 2.55 \\ \hline \end{array}$$

————

Name_____ Date _____

At the Seashore

Which number sentence (equation) can you use to find the answer for each word problem? Circle the one that is correct. Then fill in the boxes.

1. Sean collected 14 clamshells and 16 mussel shells. How many did he collect altogether?

    1.   16 - 14 = ☐☐☐☐   3.   16 + ☐☐☐☐ = 32

    2.   ☐☐☐☐ + 14 = 30   4.   Not given

2. Jessica bought a hot dog for $1.25, a soda for $.75, and french fries for $1.50.
    How much did she spend altogether?

    1. $1.25 + $.75 + ☐☐☐☐ = $5.00   3. $1.50 - $.75 = ☐☐☐☐

    2. $3.50 = $1.25 + $.75 + ☐☐☐☐   4.   Not given

3. Sean and Jessica want to ride the ferris wheel on the amusement pier.
    A ticket costs $.25, and 5 tickets are needed to ride the ferris wheel.
    How much will it cost each of them to ride?

    1.   25 x 5 = 125   3.   5 x $.25 = $1.25

    2.   5 + 5 = 10   4.   Not given

Name_____ **Date** _____

Root for the Fruit

1. Mr. Magic had 625 bananas. He used 382 of them in his magic act. How many bananas did he have left? To find the answer, fill in the numbers in the problem below. Then subtract.

```
    ┌──────┐
    │      │   bananas to start
  ┌─┼──────┤
  ─ │      │   bananas used
    ├──────┤
    │      │   bananas left
    └──────┘
```

2. Mr. Magic needs 367 oranges for the show tonight. He already has 284 oranges. How many more does he need? To find the answer, fill in the numbers in the problem below. Then subtract.

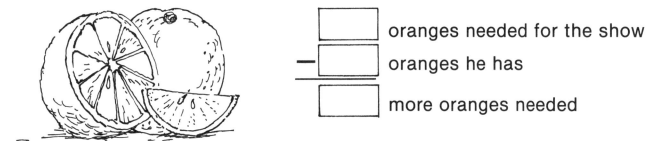

```
    ┌──────┐
    │      │   oranges needed for the show
  ┌─┼──────┤
  ─ │      │   oranges he has
    ├──────┤
    │      │   more oranges needed
    └──────┘
```

3. Mr. Magic has 448 apples. Only 172 apples have paper flowers in them. How many apples do not have paper flowers in them? To find the answer, fill in the numbers in the problem below. Then subtract.

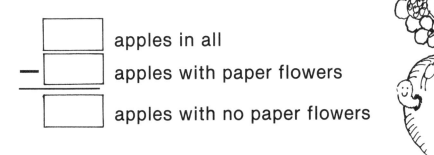

```
    ┌──────┐
    │      │   apples in all
  ┌─┼──────┤
  ─ │      │   apples with paper flowers
    ├──────┤
    │      │   apples with no paper flowers
    └──────┘
```

Name_____ Date _____

Just Passing Through

Fill in the answers.

428 − 219	457 − 286	653 − 324	366 − 195	872 − 481	993 − 628

517 − 162	936 − 741	284 − 158	736 − 583	635 − 187	345 − 279

921 − 536	873 − 628

764 − 297	626 − 328

416 − 388	527 − 178

Name_____   Date _____

56

Rabbit Snack

Magic Marty had 241 carrots. He wanted to make them disappear in his act. But his rabbits ate 158 of the carrots. Circle the problem that would help you find out how many carrots Magic Marty had left. Then solve all the problems.

$$\begin{array}{r} 617 \\ -\ 257 \\ \hline \end{array} \qquad \begin{array}{r} 562 \\ -\ 384 \\ \hline \end{array} \qquad \begin{array}{r} 624 \\ -\ 247 \\ \hline \end{array} \qquad \begin{array}{r} 437 \\ -\ 189 \\ \hline \end{array} \qquad \begin{array}{r} 510 \\ -\ 376 \\ \hline \end{array}$$

$$\begin{array}{r} 692 \\ -\ 489 \\ \hline \end{array} \qquad \begin{array}{r} 241 \\ -\ 158 \\ \hline \end{array} \qquad \begin{array}{r} 728 \\ -\ 337 \\ \hline \end{array} \qquad \begin{array}{r} 835 \\ -\ 559 \\ \hline \end{array} \qquad \begin{array}{r} 964 \\ -\ 186 \\ \hline \end{array}$$

Name _____ **Date** _____

Take a Bow

Fill in the answers.

325	558	272	716	927
− 187	− 379	− 176	− 198	− 248

631	943	363	472	654
− 254	− 556	− 275	− 193	− 269

Name_____ Date _____

Magic Paper Trick

1. Magic Marty cut a paper into 536 pieces. He dropped 387 pieces on the floor. How many pieces did not fall on the floor? To find the answer fill in the numbers in the problem below. Then subtract.

☐	pieces to start
— ☐	pieces on the floor
☐	pieces not on the floor

MAGIC TRICK!
Here's how to cut a hole BIGGER than your piece of paper!

fold the paper in half...

2. Magic Marty cut another paper into 425 pieces. A sudden wind blew 279 pieces away. How many pieces did he have left? To find out, fill in the numbers in the problem below. Then subtract.

☐	pieces to start
— ☐	pieces that blew away
☐	pieces left

then cut slashes like this...

do not cut
Then cut through the fold but do not cut the top or bottom...
do not cut

3. The last 924 times Magic Marty tried this trick, it did not work 857 times. How many times did the trick work? To find the answer, fill in the numbers in the problem below. Then subtract.

☐	times in all
— ☐	times it did not work
☐	times it worked

open it up and...

Now the hole is BIGGER than the paper!

Name _____ Date _____

Crossword Math

Solve the number problems to complete the crossword puzzle.

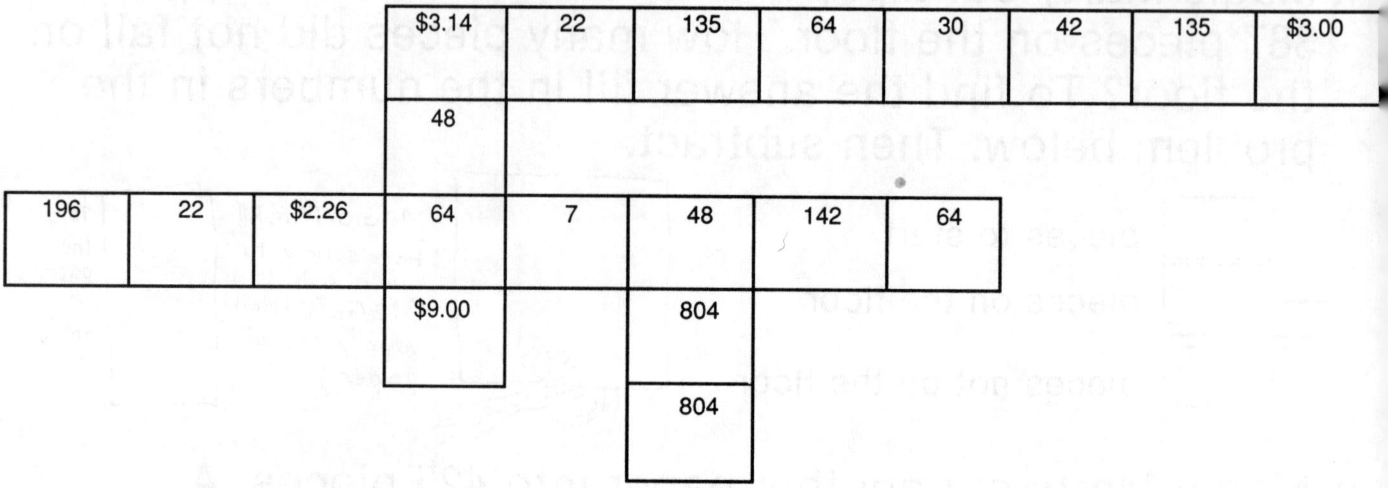

$3.14	22	135	64	30	42	135	$3.00
			48				

196	22	$2.26	64	7	48	142	64
			$9.00		804		
					804		

M.
$2.09
+ 1.05
———

U.
36
− 14
———

S.
413
− 217
———

I.
19
8
+ 3
———

A.
15
27
+ 6
———

B.
$5.29
− 3.03
———

P.
14
x 3
———

L.
27
x 5
———

D.
402
x 2
———

T.
29
+ 35
———

C.
119
+ 23
———

R.
54
− 47
———

H.
$10.99
− 1.99
———

Y.
$2.25
+ .75
———

Name_____ Date _____

Money Matters

To *reduce* a price means to make the price lower, or less. When an item goes on sale, the price is reduced. **Read each problem carefully. Write down the original price. Write down the sale or reduced price. Subtract to find the difference.**

1. A basketball that usually sells for $10.99 is reduced by $1.99. What is the new price of the basketball?

   _____

2. Jackie wants a desk that sells for $125.00. It is put on sale for $110.00. How much money does Jackie save by buying the desk on sale?

   _____

3. If a $15.00 hat is reduced by $3.00, what is the new price of the hat?

   _____

4. Miranda wants to make a new coat. The wool cloth she wants to buy was originally $21.98 a yard. The cloth is now on sale for $18.00 a yard. How much money will Miranda save on each yard of the reduced-price wool cloth?

   _____

5. *Challenge:* If Miranda needs 5 yards of wool cloth to make her coat, how much will the coat cost her at the sale price?

   _____

Name_____ **Date** _____

Let's Have a Party

Read each word problem. Think about what is being asked. Write a number sentence or sentences to solve the problem on the line. Put your final answer in the box.

1. Carmen is having a birthday party. She is inviting ten friends. Six of the guests are girls. How many boys will be at Carmen's party?

   _____

2. Carmen wants to stuff her birthday piñata with enough candy so that each one of her guests will get four pieces. How many pieces of candy does Carmen need?

   _____

3. Carmen's mother cuts the birthday cake into twenty slices. Each guest has one slice, and Carmen has two. How many slices are left?

   _____

Name_____ **Date** _____

Birthday Balloons

Draw a line from the word problems to the balloons where you can discover the right answers. Write your answers in numbers and words.

1. Carmen is shopping for birthday-party favors. At the store, she finds that a rubber ball costs $1.52. A yo-yo costs $1.85. How much more is the yo-yo than the rubber ball?

   _____

2. Her mother, Mrs. Garcia, buys paper plates for $2.49, paper cups for $1.39, and paper napkins for 99 cents. She gives the clerk $5.00. How much change does the clerk give Mrs. Garcia?

   _____

3. Carmen needs 40 pieces of candy for her birthday piñata. Each piece of candy costs a nickel. How much will the candy cost altogether?

   _____

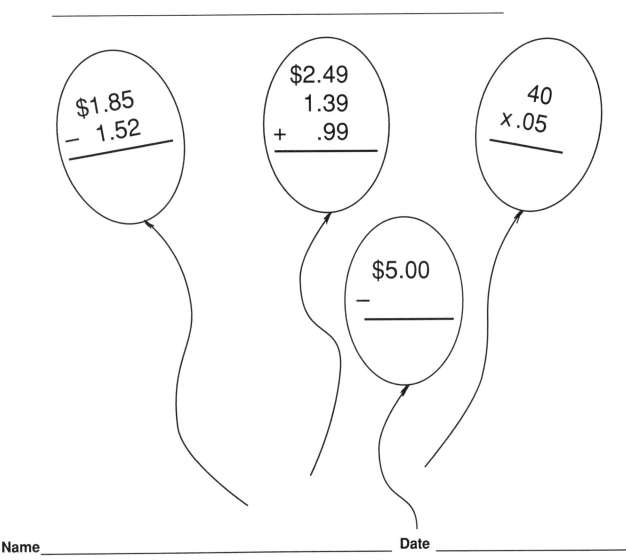

Name_____ Date _____

What's for Dinner?

Write number sentences to find the answers to the questions.
Write your final answer in words and numbers.

Mr. Green is shopping for dinner. He wants to serve lamb chops, baked potatoes, and asparagus. There are six people in the Green family. Mr. Green figures that each one will eat one chop, one potato, and four stalks of asparagus.

1. How many chops and potatoes does Mr. Green buy?

    _____

2. How many stalks of asparagus does Mr. Green buy?

    _____

3. How many food items does Mr. Green buy altogether?

    _____

4. Mr. Green's son Brian hates asparagus, so he doesn't eat any.
    His daughter Jennifer eats only two stalks. Everyone else eats
    all their asparagus. How many stalks of asparagus are left over?

    _____

Name_____ Date _____

Mother's Day

Antoine wants to buy his mother a gift and a card. He has $7.50 to spend. When he goes to the store, he finds two cards he likes. One costs $1.75 and the other costs $2.25. Then he finds a paperback book for $3.95, and a music tape for $5.99, and a pair of earrings for $6.50.

Use number sentences (equations) to answer 1, 2, 3, and 5.

1. If Antoine buys the less-expensive card and the paperback book, how much will he spend?

   _____

2. If he chooses the more-expensive card and the earrings, how much will it be?

   _____

3. If he picks the music tape and the more-expensive card, how much will it be?

   _____

4. Of choices 1, 2, or 3, which one can Antoine afford? _____

5. Antoine is unhappy because he doesn't have enough money to buy his mother what he really wants. He goes home and asks his father for a loan. How much does Antoine need to borrow to buy the more-expensive card and the earrings?

   _____

Name_____ **Date** _____

Dinosaur Doings

Follow the directions in each word problem. You will need your crayons.

207    $4.71

34   51

1. Jennifer spent $5.29 on two dinosaur toys. Her mother gave her $10.00.
    How much money does Jennifer have left to spend? Color the dinosaur
    with the correct answer *red*.

2. Apatosaurus needs to eat 122 plants each day to live. He ate 23 at breakfast
    and 48 at lunch. How many more plants does he have to eat at dinner?
    Color the dinosaur with the correct answer *blue*.

3. Tyrannosaurus Rex has two rows of teeth. Each row has 132 teeth.
    If 57 teeth fall out, how many teeth would Tyrannosaurus Rex have
    left? Color the dinosaur with the correct answer *green*.

4. Allosaurus and Stegosaurus were in 86 fights in all. Allosaurus was in
    26 fights. But Stegosaurus had 60 fights. How many more fights does
    Allosaurus have to get into to equal Stegosaurus' fights? Color the
    dinosaur with the correct answer *yellow*.

Name_____   **Date** _____

The Food Market

Write a multiplication problem(s) after each word problem to solve the following.

1. Chelsea filled 3 bags with 6 apples each. How many apples did Chelsea buy?

    _____

2. Stephanie wants each member of her family to have 2 ears of corn. If there are 4 people in Stephanie's family, how much corn should she buy?

    _____

3. Raoul found 4 bunches of grapes. Two bunches had 9 grapes each. The other two bunches had 6 grapes each. How many grapes were on all 4 bunches?

    _____

4. Steven bought 4 six-packs of soda. How many cans of soda did Steven buy?

    _____

5. Each party guest said he or she could eat 5 mini-pizza bagels. If there are 12 party guests, how many pizza bagels should Laura buy?

    _____

Name_____ **Date** _____

Time Travels

Use the clock to help you solve these time word problems.

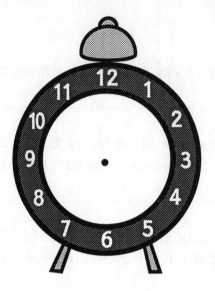

1. Julian practices violin for 30 minutes every day after dinner. He finishes dinner at 5:30 p.m. When does he finish practicing violin?

   _____

2. Sharon walks her dog for 45 minutes. If she begins her walk at 3:15 p.m., what time does she finish?

   _____

3. Vince is on the swim team. He practices swimming from 6:30 a.m. to 7:00 a.m. and from 3:00 p.m. to 3:30 p.m. How many hours does Vince practice swimming each day?

   _____

4. Mother's family always eats dinner at 6:15 p.m. If they take 30 minutes to eat, when do they finish eating dinner?

   _____

5. It takes Robert 40 minutes to mow the lawn. If he starts to mow it at 5:00 p.m., when will he be finished?

   _____

Time Tricks

Use the clock to help you solve these time word problems.

1. Baseball practice starts at four o'clock in the afternoon. Mike was twenty minutes late. When did Mike get to practice?

    _____

2. Yolanda's favorite show begins at 7:30 p.m. Mama says she must finish her homework first. If Yolanda finishes dinner at 6:15 p.m. and begins her homework right away, how much time doe she have to do her assignment?

    _____

3. Rebecca's school bus picks her up at 15 minutes after eight in the morning. It takes Rebecca forty-five minutes to get ready. What is the latest Rebecca can get up?

    _____

4. Juan loves to draw. He draws for twenty minutes before breakfast. Then he draws for forty minutes after supper. How much times does Juan spend drawing each day?

    _____

Name_____ **Date** _____

TV Time Troubles

Read the paragraph carefully. Then solve the following word problems.

Jonathan is allowed to watch one hour of television on school nights. He can watch three hours of TV on days that there is no school. Sometimes his parents let him "borrow" TV time from the next day so that he can watch longer on a school night. This is important to Jonathan because he loves sports.

1. On Monday night, Jonathan wants to watch "The Stupids" for a half hour, and "America's Silliest Teachers" for 30 minutes. How long does Jonathan want to watch TV?

   _____

2. Jonathan's favorite hockey team is playing on Tuesday night. The game will take two hours. On Wednesday night, his mother wants to watch a two-hour ballet. Jonathan hates ballet. What can Jonathan do to watch the hockey game on Tuesday?

   _____

   _____

3. "Giant Mutant Superheroes" is Jonathan's favorite cartoon show. It is on from 9:30 a.m. to 10:30 a.m. on Saturday. Later that day, a basketball-bloopers show is on from 2:00 p.m. to 3:30 p.m. Jonathan wants to watch that, too. He also wants to see a movie that starts at 7:30 p.m. and ends at 9:00 p.m. How many hours of TV does Jonathan want to watch? Is that more or less than he is allowed?

   _____

Name_____ **Date** _____

Food Fun

Use the pictures to help solve the fraction word problems. A fraction is part of something. The bottom number tells the total number of pieces in the whole item. The top number tells the pieces asked for in the word problem. **Choose your answers from the fractions in the box and write them on the lines.**

1. Jose and Raymond share a pizza. The pizza is cut into 8 pieces. Each boy eats one half of the pizza. Choose the fraction which shows how much pizza Jose eats.

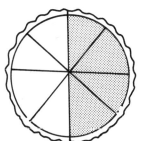

_____

2. Sandra bakes an apple pie. She divides it into three equal pieces. One piece she gives to her mother, and one piece she gives to her friend. How much pie does Sandra have left for herself? Choose the fraction which shows how much pie Sandra has left.

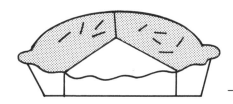

_____

3. John, Michael, Susan, and Sara share a foot-long hero sandwich. They divide the sandwich into four equal pieces. How much of the sandwich does Michael eat? Choose the fraction which shows Michael's piece.

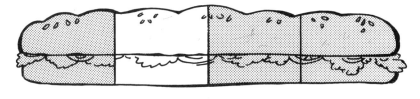

_____

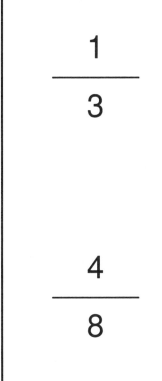

$$\frac{1}{3}$$

$$\frac{4}{8}$$

$$\frac{1}{4}$$

Name_____ **Date** _____

Measurement Madness

Lindsey and Mark want to help clean the house. Use the chart to help the children do their chores. **Be sure to label your answers.**

```
 2 cups   = 1 pint
 2 pints  = 1 quart
 4 quarts = 1 gallon
12 inches = 1 foot
 3 feet   = 1 yard
```

1. Mark is going to mop the floor. He has to mix 1 gallon of water with 2 cups of liquid floor cleaner. How many *pints* of liquid will Mark have altogether?

   _____

2. Lindsey wants to wash windows. She needs 1 gallon of total liquid. If 1 *quart* of the liquid is vinegar, how much of the gallon is water?

   _____

3. Mark and Lindsey are wiping down the kitchen countertops. If one counter measures 2 feet and another counter measures 4 feet, how many *yards* of countertop do Mark and Lindsey have to clean?

   _____

4. Mark and Lindsey's mom wants to put up a new kitchen curtain. She asks the children to measure the length of the window. The window measures 48 inches long. How many *feet* long will the new curtain have to be?

   _____

Name_____ **Date** _____

Roman Rules

You may see Roman numbers on clocks. Sometimes Roman numbers are used at the beginning of chapters in books. Here's how you read Roman numbers:

$$I = 1 \qquad V = 5 \qquad X = 10$$

Add the letters when they are the same: $\quad II = 1 + 1 = 2$

Add the letters when the larger value comes first:
$VI = 5 + 1 = 6$
$XII = 10 + 1 + 1 = 12$

Subtract the letters when the smaller value comes first:
$IV = 5 - 1 = 4$
$IX = 10 - 1 = 9$

Read the Roman numbers. Write the answers in word form. Put one letter of the word on each line. The letters in the boxes spell out something we like to have at the beach. (The first one is done for you.)

Roman	Word (boxed letter)
V	[F] I V E
IV	__ __ [box] __
X	__ __ [box]
I	[box] __ __
VII	__ __ __ __ [box]
XII	[box] __ __ __ __ __
XVIII	__ __ __ [box] __ __ __ __
XV	__ __ __ __ [box] __ __
VI	[box] __ __
III	__ [box] __ __ __
II	__ __ [box]
XIII	__ __ __ [box] __ __ __ __
XI	__ __ [box] __ __ __

Name_____ Date _____

Money Talks

1. Luis gets $2.00 allowance each Friday. He earns $3.00 each Saturday doing chores for Mrs. Gonzalez. **How many weeks** does Luis have to save to buy a new cap for $8.99?

_____

2. **How many weeks** does he have to save to buy a CD that costs $10.99?

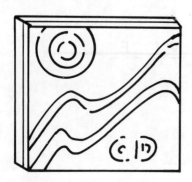

_____

3. Luis wants new sneakers that cost $75.00. His mother has promised to pay $50.00. **How many weeks** does Luis have to save until he has enough to buy the sneakers?

_____

Name_____   Date _____